BRER RABBIT
AND THE GREAT RACE
AND
HOW BRER RABBIT LOST HIS TAIL

Illustrated by Lesley Smith

AWARD PUBLICATIONS LIMITED

A Read With Me Story Book

Brer Rabbit

Coat

Brer Fox

Rock

Pictured on this page are some of the animals and things featured in this story. Encourage the children to whom you are reading to SEE and SAY the word for each.

Then, as you read the story to them and you come to a picture in place of a word, pause each time for the children to SEE and SAY.

Children love to participate in this kind of storytelling and the SEE and SAY storybooks will become their first choice for reading fun.

Brer Terrapin

Fish

ISBN 1-84135-053-2

Copyright © 2001 Award Publications Limited

First published 2001 by Award Publications Limited,
27 Longford Street, London NW1 3DZ

Printed in Malaysia

Mrs Terrapin

River

Brer Hedgehog

Animals

Post

Tail

BRER RABBIT
AND THE GREAT RACE

Brer Rabbit was always playing tricks

on the other , but sometimes

they played tricks on him.

One day  was walking along

the road when he met .

"Hello, slowcoach," said .

 thought  was very

rude, so he said, "I may be slow on

land but I am a good swimmer."

 knew that although

could swim, he was no faster in the

 than he was

on the land.

"I will have a race with you," said  . "I will run on the land and you can swim in the  ."

All the  helped to mark out a racetrack, five miles along the bank of the  .

At the end of each mile the  put up a  and on the last one they tied a ribbon across the  .

"This is where the end of the race will be," said  .

So  went home laughing as he thought of how easily he would beat  the next day.

But he didn't know that  was going to play a trick on him.

Very early the next morning
and  came along with their four

children.

When they had taken off their hats, all

the terrapins looked alike.

 waited at the start, and each

of the children hid at one of the

 s along the  bank.

 hid at the winning-.

"Ready, steady, go!"

called . As

dived into the

,

raced away

along the

bank.

As  arrived

at each mile-  ,

he was surprised

to see that

was swimming down

the  in front of him.

"I didn't think  could swim

so fast!" he panted.

When  reached the end of the race, he was amazed to find that  was already waiting at the winning-  .

"Did you lose your way?" asked , and all the other

laughed at the trick they had played.  could not understand

how he had lost the race, but he was

careful not to laugh at  next

time he saw him!

HOW BRER RABBIT
LOST HIS TAIL

Many years ago Brer Rabbit had

a long and bushy  , just like a

squirrel's.  was very proud of

his  .

One bright winter morning he met

 walking along carrying some

fine  on a string.

"Those look good,"

said . "Where did

you catch them?"

"I caught them in the 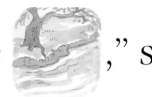," said . "There are more there if you want to catch some!"

"I would like to catch some ," said . "Can you tell me how to do it?"

 thought that he could play a trick on .

"All you have to do," he said, "is to sit with your  in the  tonight, and when you get up in the morning your  will be covered in ."

"My goodness, that sounds very easy!" said . "I will go home and get ready to catch some ."

 went

back to his house

to get ready.

He packed a  with a hot

drink and lots of juicy  so he

would not be hungry.

Later that evening he put on his

big , and his , and put his

red woolly  on his head, so that

would be warm too.

"Now I am ready to go and catch

lots of !" said  ,

and off he went

to the  .

It was very, very cold that night.

 sat on a in the

with his  in the icy water.

By the morning poor  felt

very tired and quite frozen.

"I must be catching a fine lot of

 with my ," he said, to

cheer himself up.

"Now I will see how many  I have caught," said  and he tried to pull his  out of the 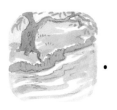.

But  found that his  had frozen in the  and as he got up it snapped off.

" has played a trick on me," said  as he looked at his white fluffy stump. "I have no  and no  either!"

And that is why all rabbits now

have little white fluffy bobtails

instead of long, bushy  s.